P9-CKW-784

WITHDRAWN

WITHDRAWN

The
NEAT LINE
Scribbling Through Mother Goose

Pamela Duncan Edwards

Illustrated by

Diana Cain Bluthenthal

KATHERINE TEGEN BOOKS
An Imprint of HarperCollins Publishers

The Neat Line
Text copyright © 2005 by Pamela Duncan Edwards
Illustrations copyright © 2005 by Diana Cain Bluthenthal
Manufactured in China by South China Printing Company Ltd.
All rights reserved.
www.harperchildrens.com

Library of Congress Cataloging-in-Publication Data
Edwards, Pamela Duncan.
The neat line / by Pamela Duncan Edwards ;
illustrations by Diana Cain Bluthenthal.—1st ed.   p.   cm.
Summary: A young scribble matures into a neat line,
then wriggles into a book of nursery rhymes, where it
transforms itself into different objects to assist
the characters it meets there.
ISBN 0-06-623970-2 — ISBN 0-06-623971-0 (lib. bdg.)
[1. Line (Art)—Fiction.   2. Characters in literature—Fiction.
3. Nursery rhymes—Fiction.]   I. Bluthenthal, Diana Cain, ill.
II. Title.   PZ7 .E26365 Ne 2005
[E]—dc21   2002153424   CIP   AC

Typography by Carla Weise
1 2 3 4 5 6 7 8 9 10
❖
First Edition

For
Jackson Robert Edwards,
who is busy learning
how to make neat lines.
Love, Grandma
—P.D.E.

Which is better:
The smallest good deed,
Or the greatest intention?
To those who help others.
—D.C.B.

Once upon a time there was a scribble.
The scribble was only a baby.

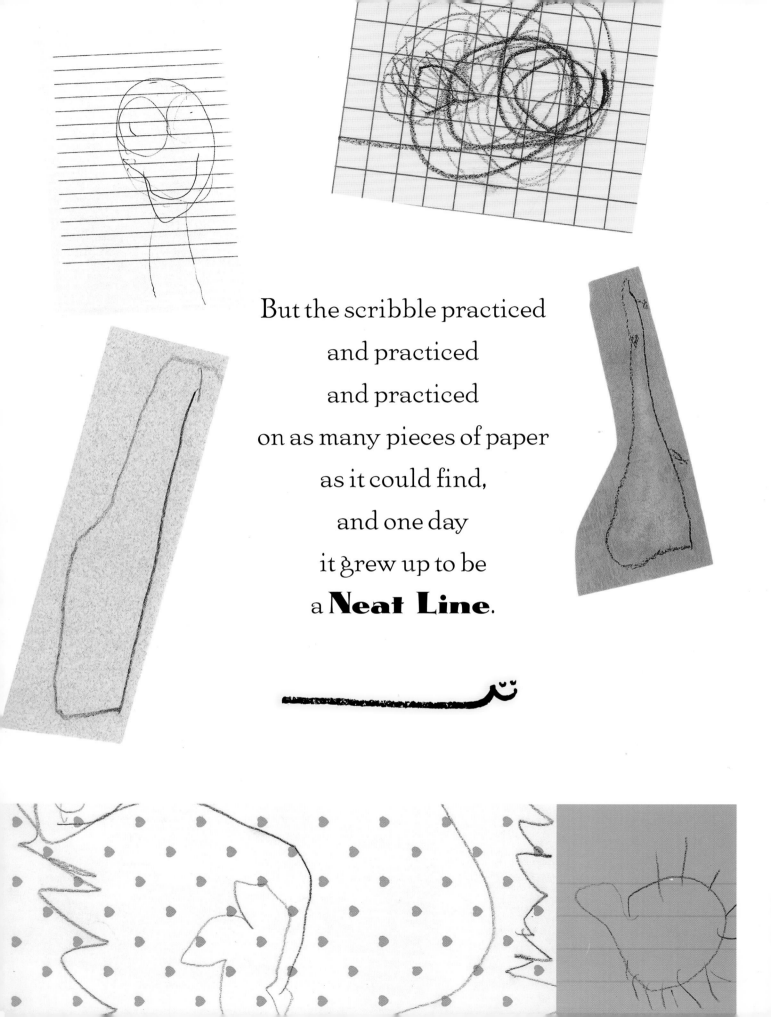

But the scribble practiced
and practiced
and practiced
on as many pieces of paper
as it could find,
and one day
it grew up to be
a **Neat Line**.

i O m i
I a m

I am on eat lxine

I am a neat line

I am a neat line

I am a neat line.

I am a Neat Line!

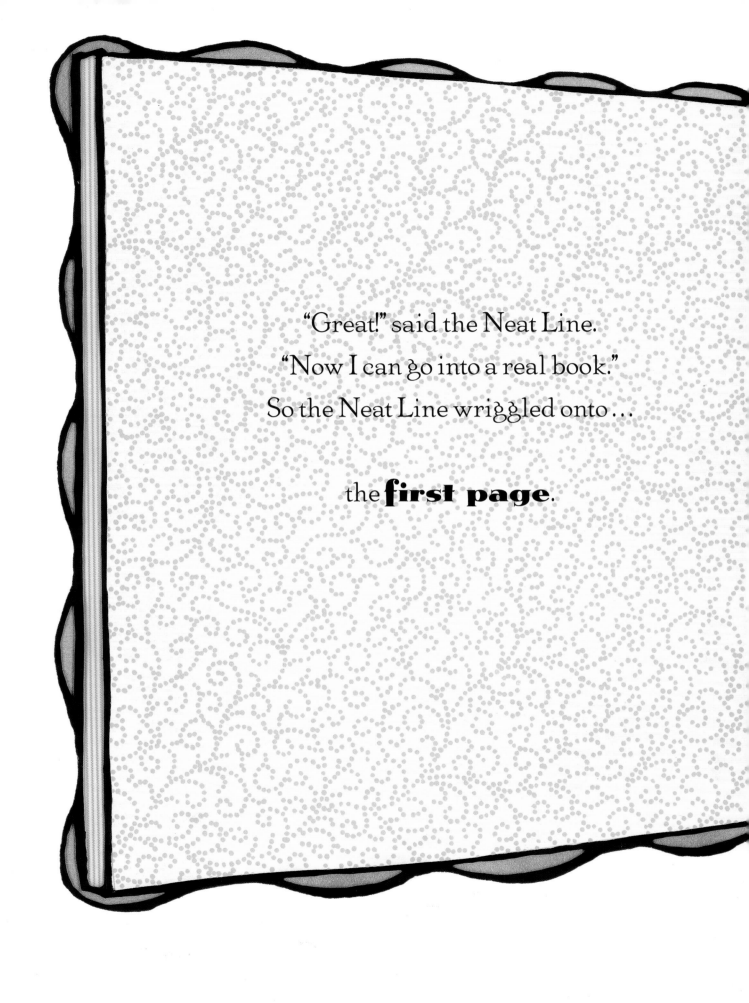

"Great!" said the Neat Line.
"Now I can go into a real book."
So the Neat Line wriggled onto...

the **first page**.

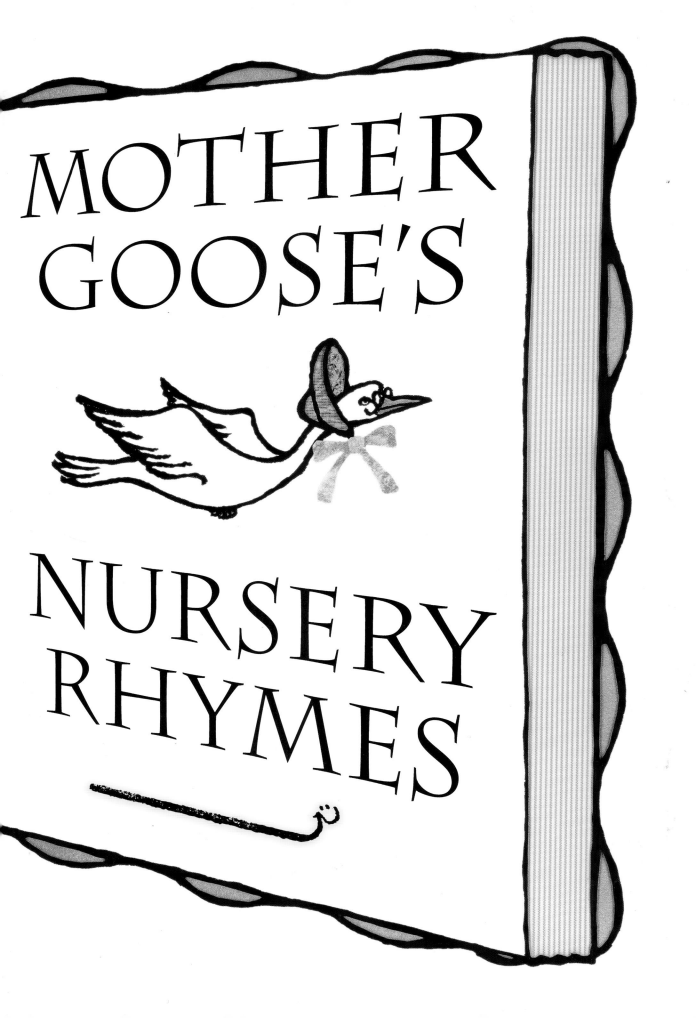

A little boy sat under a haystack.

"Boo, hoo!" cried the little boy.

"What's the matter?" asked the Neat Line.

"I'm supposed to look after the sheep and the cows," sobbed the little boy. "But I fell asleep, and now look at the mess I'm in. I don't know what to do."

Little Boy Blue, come blow your horn,
The sheep's in the meadow, the cow's in the corn.
Where is the boy who looks after the sheep?
He's under the haystack, fast asleep.

"Leave it to me," said the Neat Line, and quick as a flash, it drew itself into a horn.

"Toot! Toot!" went the little boy. The sheep trotted into their pen, and the cows lumbered into the cow pasture.

"That was so clever of you," said the little boy.
He went back to the haystack and fell asleep again.

"No problem," said the Neat Line, and it wriggled onto ...

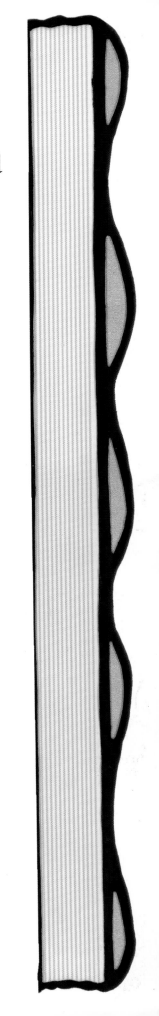

the **next page**.

Bang! Crash! Rattle!

"Ouch!" cried a voice. "That hurt!"

"What's the matter?" asked the Neat Line.

"The grass is so slippery," wailed the girl.

"Jack and I keep rolling down."

Jack and Jill went up the hill
To fetch a pail of water.
Jack fell down and broke his crown,
And Jill came tumbling after.

"Leave it to me," said the Neat Line,
and quick as a flash, it drew itself
into a pathway leading up
the hill.

Jack and Jill ran up
the pathway and filled
their pail with water.

"Thanks a lot," said Jack when they reached the bottom of the hill. "I was so tired of Granny wrapping my bumps in vinegar and brown paper."

"Glad to help," said the Neat Line, and it wriggled onto ...

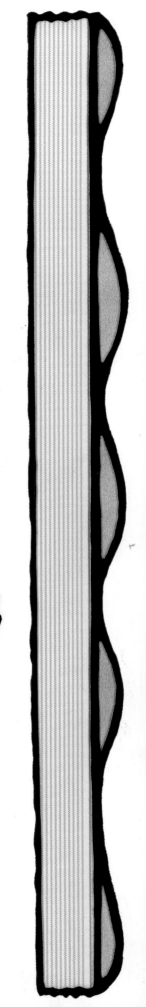

the **next page**.

"This is a pretty garden,"
said the Neat Line.

"That's what you think!"
said a flower.

"What's the matter?" asked
the Neat Line.

"Mary's in a bad mood because
we didn't admire the cockleshells
she planted," said the flower.

"And she's forgotten to
water us," cried another flower.

"We're so thirsty.
We're withering away."

Mary, Mary, quite contrary,
How does your garden grow?
With silver bells and cockleshells,
And pretty maids all in a row.

"Leave it to me," said the Neat Line, and quick as flash, it drew itself into a big cloud. The cloud began to rain on the flowers.

"You saved us," cried the flowers as they soaked up the water.

"Don't mention it," said the Neat Line, and it wriggled onto ...

the **next page**.

"Go away, greedy thing," yelled a little girl.

"Who, me?" asked the Neat Line. "What did I do?"

"I don't mean you," said the little girl. "I'm talking to that thief of a spider."

"Here I come," called the spider.

Little Miss Muffet sat on a tuffet,
Eating her curds and whey.
Along came a spider,
And sat down beside her,
And frightened Miss Muffet away.

"Leave it to me," said the Neat Line, and
quick as a flash, it drew itself into a big bird.
"Eek! I'm leaving!" screamed the spider.
"It's dangerous around here!"

"Thank you," said the little girl. "This is the first time in ages I've been able to finish a meal."

"All in a day's work," said the Neat Line as it wriggled onto …

the **next page**.

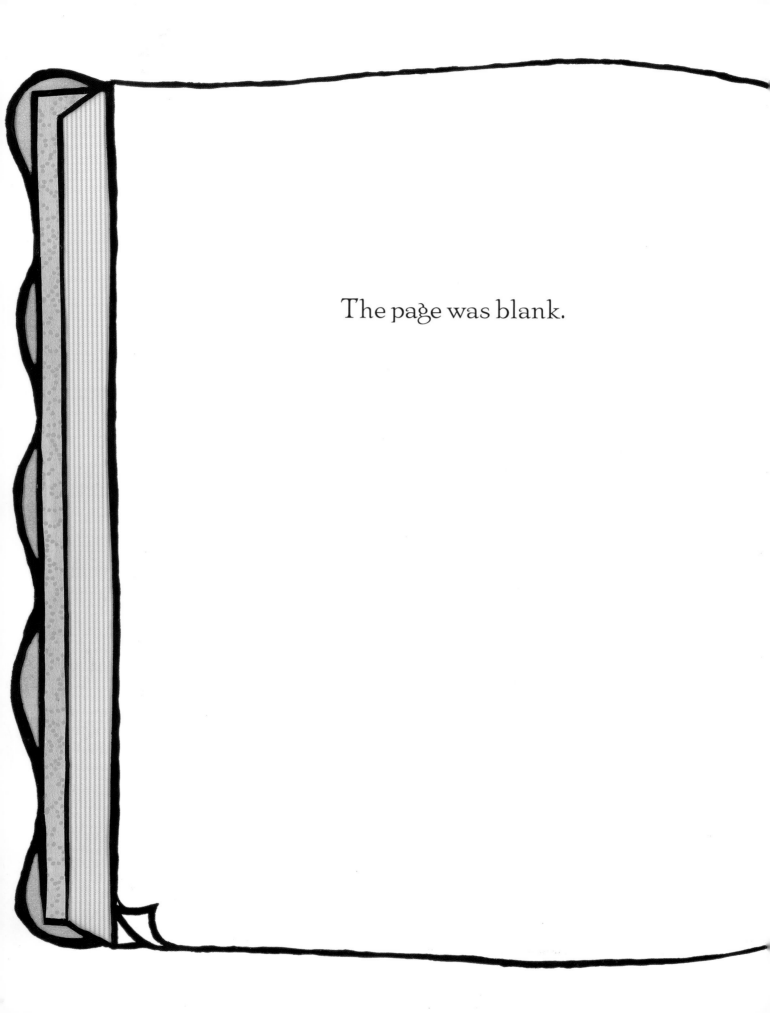

The page was blank.

"Thank goodness," said
the Neat Line. "It's very hard
work being a grown-up line."

And tiredly, the Neat Line drew itself into …

the Man in the Moon,

and switched off the light!

z z z z z

Good Night